KU-166-824

Published by Ladybird Books Ltd
Penguin Books Ltd, 80 Strand, London WC2R 0RL, England
Penguin (Group) Australia, 250 Camberwell Road, Camberwell, Victoria 3124, Australia
Penguin Group (NZ), cnr Airborne and Rosedale Roads, Albany, Auckland 1310,
New Zealand
A Penguin Company

1 3 5 7 9 10 8 6 4 2
This presentation copyright © Ladybird Books Ltd, 2006
New reproductions of Beatrix Potter's book illustrations copyright © Frederick Warne & Co.,
2002
Original text and illustrations copyright © Frederick Warne & Co., 1907

Additional illustrations by Liz Catchpole, Colin Twinn and Alex Vining

ISBN-13: 978-1-8464 6356-3
ISBN-10: 1-8464-6356-4

Printed in Italy

THE TALE OF TOM KITTEN

A SIMPLIFIED RETELLING OF THE ORIGINAL TALE BY
BEATRIX POTTER

Here are three little
kittens: Mittens,
Tom Kitten and Moppet.

One day their mother,
Mrs Tabitha Twitchit, took
them indoors to get ready
for a tea-party.

7

First she
scrubbed
their faces.
(This kitten
is Moppet.)

Then she
brushed
their fur.
(This
kitten is
Mittens.)

Then she combed their tails
and whiskers. (This kitten is
Tom.)

Mrs Tabitha Twitchit took some fine clothes out of the drawer and dressed her kittens.

The kittens found the clothes very uncomfortable. Moppet and Mittens wore white pinafores.

Tom Kitten's blue suit
was too small for him.
The buttons burst off.

Mrs Tabitha Twitchit sewed
them on again.

When they were ready, Mrs Tabitha Twitchit sent them outside to play.

"Keep your frocks clean, children," she said.

In the garden, Tom Kitten
chased a butterfly.

Moppet and Mittens fell
down on the path and made
their clothes dirty.

Then Moppet and Mittens climbed up and sat on the garden wall. "Come along, Tom," they called.

Tom Kitten's buttons had
burst off again.

Moppet and Mittens
helped Tom to climb up the
garden wall.

He lost his hat and his suit was
falling off.

As the kittens sat on the garden wall, three ducks came walking along the road. They were called the Puddle-ducks.

The Puddle-ducks put on
Tom's hat.

Moppet, Mittens and Tom
Kitten laughed so much that
they fell off the garden wall.

"Will you help us dress Tom
Kitten?" said Moppet to the
Puddle-ducks.

But one of the Puddle-ducks
put Tom Kitten's clothes
on himself!

"It is a very fine morning,"
said the Puddle-duck.

Then the three Puddle-ducks
walked off along the road
with all of the kittens' clothes.

Their feet went *pit pat,
paddle pat! Pit pat, waddle pat!*

Mrs Tabitha Twitchit found
her kittens sitting on the
garden wall with no
clothes on.

She was very angry.
She smacked those kittens,
and sent them upstairs!

When Mrs Tabitha's
friends arrived, she told
them that her kittens were
in bed with the measles.

But the kittens were not in
bed at all!

The Puddle-ducks went into a pond and the clothes all came off. They are still looking for them!